The golden leaves shimmered in the breeze. They whispered to one another, presumably sweet nothings or else top secrets, so hushed were they. Hushed yet rushed. Urgent. All passing on these clandestine messages at once. If you strained your ear perhaps you could catch the odd word. But must they all chatter at once? It made it difficult. Probably wasn't English anyway. Why would trees communicate in English? Or in any language known to man for that matter? Perhaps they were making music - some sort of chorale. Beautiful cadences, crescendos from *pianissimo* to *piano*, interspersed with the staccato pip, pip of birdsong. She took a breath, filling her lungs, saturating her haemoglobin with the tree's life-giving oxygen. What was that? Amid the rustle, the hustle and bustle, it came again. Her name. They were discussing *her*. Gossiping about her. How rude! "Flora", they murmured. Calling her. Beckoning her. She looked around. No one was there. Or not nearby anyway - there was an elderly couple at the top of the hill, peering into a flowerbed. She gingerly stepped over the low fence of wire hoops embedded in the earth. She had to crush some of the pampas grass. There was a little notice at the foot of the trunk. *Betula ermanii.* She reached out and touched the bark. To her surprise, considering the chill in the air, it was warm. She placed both palms flat against its torso. It pulsated beneath her fingers. The peeling skin blushed rose in colour.

****

AF407985

It was a grey day. In fact, it had been a grey week. Looking out, it could have been morning or evening, there being no way of telling in the sun's absence. The incontinent clouds dribbled. It was the kind of rain that causes a debate as to whether or not you actually need to put up the brolly, the seemingly light droplets almost unnoticeable until you wonder how, upon arrival at your destination, you have come to peel off a sopping wet jacket.

Flora felt sad. Perhaps things would have been different were the garden drenched in sunlight instead. There was the swing. It seemed like only yesterday that she was sitting units bright red seat shrieking "Higher! Higher!" as her mother pushed. She remembered her cousin, Paul standing in front, challenging her to bowl him over but ducking out of the way at the last minute. She could not recall ever hitting him, try as she might, stretching out her jelly-shoed feet. Apparently he had attempted a similar trick with Amy ten years earlier, but she had been horrified and it was a game never to be repeated. She was flying towards his goofy face, convinced she was going to hurt him and unable to stop. In her panic she tucked up her legs, let go of the ropes to cover her eyes and promptly fell backwards, cracking her head, the first of many bumps. Paul had got in so much trouble so it was very brave of him to play with Flora. When this tale was related to her, several years down the line, she felt a sense of shame. Five years old and Amy would put others before herself whereas Flora, at the same age, was doing her utmost to inflict injury!

The frame of the swing was rusty now and the paintwork had all but disappeared from the seat, the odd pinkish fleck here and there but otherwise only splintered wood visible. It was pretty much representative of the entire garden, tired and unloved. The pond Amy had insisted they put in, stagnant and blanketed in thick, green algae; her father's vegetable patch, once a labour of love and the source of the family's five-a-day, now reduced to a lifeless quagmire; the window of the tool shed was cracked and the creaky door swung open and shut in the wind; very occasionally half-hearted attempts at weeding were made but the result of this was simply displacement from the 'flower' beds to the patchy lawn where their decomposing piles were accompanied by heaps of rubble from goodness-knows-where. When had her parents stopped caring? Then with simultaneous pangs of guilt and fear, Flora thought that perhaps they hadn't. They were not young. They had other things to worry about.

She supposed it didn't particularly matter anyway with the sale of the property agreed. It didn't seem real yet. "The Faircloughs' Place" would revert back to impersonal, meaningless 45 Blythe Way. Would her parents be taking the sign on the gatepost with them? "If you want a guarantee, buy a toaster". Probably. If other houses had plaques of the non-blue variety they were either "Rose Cottage" or the like or "Beware of the Dog", not a display of the occupants' philosophy on life. She hadn't understood it as a child.

The slow bobbing of a wood pigeon, that cow of the bird world, caught her eye. The rain had brought the worms to the surface. They could have done with this weather last summer when she had her kids worm-charming. A shower probably worked better than any of their methods. Still, they enjoyed themselves and hopefully learnt something. Just above the pigeon, a single, tightly furled pink bud was stubbornly sprouting on the cherry tree. Flora smiled and turned from the window.

As she approached the front door of the flat, Flora's heart sunk. There was the familiar thud of Cassie's music. She actually considered turning round and going back out again, but it had been a long day and she didn't really have anywhere else to go. She put her key in the lock, her temperature rising. She hated being angry but it was happening with increasing frequency. She just wanted to sit with her feet up and catch up with the papers. Catch up with her thoughts. She had always imagined that she would have her own place by now. Scratch that: she distinctly remembered saying in her French oral (to demonstrate use of the future tense) that she would travel the world, be a doctor, marry at twenty-four and have the first of her two children at twenty-five. Hmm. Well, she'd been to Thailand for three weeks. And hated it.

She put down her rucksack and kicked off her shoes, replacing them with a pair of oversized fuzzy green socks. Was it too early to get into her pyjamas? Flora would quite happily have a wardrobe comprised entirely of pyjamas. Tiger came bounding up the passageway, mewing. His needle-like talons punctured her trousers and slotted neatly into the holes in her leg he had made yesterday.

"Ouch! Little monster!" she yelped, unhooking his claws.

She lifted him up in front of her face, his back legs dangling.

"What are we going to do with you, hey?" she smiled.

No wonder he was so naughty, she was a hopeless disciplinarian. She looked into his big green eyes. His pupils grew wide. He wriggled a bit before giving her a playful bop on the nose.

Tiger actually belonged to Cassie but, despite all the toys and treats she had offered him in the early days, he didn't seem to be aware of this fact. He spent his very first night in the flat curled up on Flora's pillow right next to her face. And every night from then on. Flora used to put him on Cassie's bed out of guilt but he wasn't having it. She couldn't help but think that perhaps this was on account of Cassie mistaking him for a girl and christening him Tigerlily. She had tried to explain that ginger cats were always toms but Cassie had insisted that he looked far too pretty to be a boy and, anyway, he had been sold to her as female. Even now though, seven months down the line, she would call him Lily. He only answered to Tiger though. Poor thing, it must be a struggle to assert one's masculinity with a girl's name and having been given the snip.

The two of them went through to the little kitchen and Flora switched the kettle on. Thanks to her flatmate's disregard for the environment, there was no need to add any water: Cassie always filled it to the brim, no matter how much she needed. A used teabag lay on a crumbly plate by the sink. Did Flora growl out loud? Cassie didn't drink tea so Kehinde must have been round. Was he still round?

"No PJs yet then" she told Tiger who was circling her legs.

Her pyjamas were perfectly respectable and Kehinde was no stranger but Flora just didn't feel comfortable being in her nightwear when there were guests.

She swilled the teabag around in the steaming water, then fished it out with the spoon and carried it over to the bin. It was full. Tiger reattached himself to her legs and the teabag plopped onto the floor. This made him retract his claws. He was a very suspicious animal, seemingly convinced that everyone and everything was out to get him. Put anything out of the ordinary in his bowl and he'd be hissing at it. He puffed up his tail and spat at the soggy disc, before tapping it gingerly with his paw. Failing to get a reaction, he crept round it three times before crouching down and wiggling his bottom in the air. Then came the pounce. The bag was punctured and tealeaves stained the cream tiles.

"Flora, hi!"
"Oh, hi, Kenny, I didn't realise you were here" she lied.

With a turn of the head so very slight, he flashed her one of his big trademark grins, revealing an incongruous set of perfect pearly teeth. He wasn't falling for that.

The two stood awkwardly opposite each other. Looking at Kehinde as he leant into the doorframe, Flora changed her mind. *She* stood awkwardly. He stood. It was only a tiny kitchen and, with no windows, relied on the light from the living room. The flat always seemed so much smaller when Kehinde was there, now more than ever with his huge might taking up the entire doorway. His right arm was stretched above his head, his fingers slowly stroking the woodwork. The stretch had caused his shirt to come untucked, revealing a small triangle of firm flesh, dark hair snaking up to his naval. His left hand was curled around his book. It was so stuffed with pieces of paper and brightly coloured post-its, that it could not be closed flat. He was wearing a shiny red tie. He was still smiling.

Tiger launched himself at Kehinde's shoe, gripping the lace with his teeth and rolling onto his back.

"Excuse me" Flora mumbled, reaching across to the light switch.

Kehinde laughed, bent down and scooped up the kitten in one hand.

"What do you girls feed Lily?"

Flora winced.

"Jumping beans?"

She knelt to wipe up the burst teabag, very aware that her drink was getting cold.

"Oh no, Cassie spent ages cleaning up the kitchen this morning. She knows how tired and stressed you get with work. She even threw out all the past-it food from the fridge" he beamed.

Flora felt a pang of guilt. She hadn't even noticed. In fact, she had been annoyed. If she had thought about it though, she would have realised that that was the reason the bin was full when she had only just emptied it.

"And after she'd cleaned, she made you a lasagne. Vegetarian. I chopped the onion."

That would explain the tomatoey pans in the sink Flora could see as she rinsed the cloth. So, she had a reputation for being stressed out? Cassie was a primary school teacher too. They met at university. Flora often forgot they did the same job; Cassie was so calm and relaxed and rarely even mentioned work.

"Hey, Flora! You see what I did? *And* I made you a lasagne"
"I chopped the onion"
"You just need to put it in the oven"

Sometimes Cassie reminded her of one of her pupils. She couldn't stay cross with her. That was the thing with Cassie: you could be really mad at her when she wasn't there, but, even if you were planning on having words, when face to face, the anger melted away and you just felt guilty.

"She means well" her mother would say on the phone as Flora grumbled.

"Anyway, we're off out. Have a good one!" Cassie tugged Kehinde by the elbow. He put Tiger down and kissed her on the forehead. "Oh?"

Kehinde tapped his book, his favourite book.

"Prayer meeting followed by Bible study"
"Bye Lily!" Cassie called from the front door.
"Bye Flora!" Cassie called from the other side of the front door. An afterthought.

Flora shuffled into the living room and flopped onto the sofa. There was no sign of the newspaper. It must have been tidied. She took a sip of her tea. She had forgotten the milk.

A key turned in the lock.

"Forgot to say: your sister called round this morning. She didn't want to come in. No message. See ya!"

Flora choked on her tea. Her *sister*?

*

Her sister. Amy. Here. At her flat. What? How? Cassie must have made a mistake. Or she, Flora, had misunderstood. Amy had called, phoned. But that was unlikely. Scratch that, impossible - they had no landline. Amy. Here. At her flat. It didn't make sense.

*

Little people all around. Thirty of them. Little people, big noise. Squeals. Squawks. Shrieks. Laughter. Tears. Rage. A melting pot of emotions, nothing held back, all on display. Little people. She didn't like to call them children - it somehow diminished them. They were complex beings right from the start. Not that Flora had much experience of babies, herself the baby of the family and no young cousins, nieces or nephews. That was a funny thought - Amy with a baby, a mother. Or what about herself? How would she fare as a parent? She went through a broody phase a couple of years back but that had passed. The job will have done that. She looked around. Glitter everywhere. Sand. Paint. Stickiness. She was a scientist was she not? How did she end up in charge of a room full to bursting with little people? Was she over-qualified or under? Under, she decided as a pool of warm, yellow liquid grew about the feet of a bespectacled cherub. He didn't move. Looked surprised. She didn't move. There were fisticuffs in the Home Corner. The volume rose. The room spun around her. She was hot. Everything was a blur.

"Mrs Fairclough, Charlie's done a wee!"

She'd been married off. She blinked a few times and the world swam back into focus. Little fingers were tugging at her sleeve. Persistent. She had to get a grip. She was an adult. These little lives were in her care. More than that, she was there to educate them, to impart her wisdom. Where was Magda? Probably just as well she had disappeared, the last thing she needed was a witness to this chaos, to her lack of authority.

"Mrs Fairclough!"
"Right!" She clapped her hands. "Everyone stop what you're doing and listen!"

Just one pupil seemed to have taken notice. Asma immediately put down the doll she had been nursing and pressed a digit to her lips. You weren't supposed to have favourites but Asma was hers. She couldn't help it. It wasn't just that she was well-behaved, obedient. She was interested, eager to learn, gentle-natured. Flora smiled weakly in her direction. She clapped her hands again. She had no control in this classroom whatsoever. How did she let things escalate to this level? Was it not just a minute ago that the children were sitting at their desks, deeply involved in the creation of collages of the seasons? Where had her mind drifted off to this time? She moved swiftly about the room, pushing tables back into position, picking up detritus from the floor and gently pressing little bodies onto miniature chairs. She fetched a mop for Charlie. She could do this. She was competent. You were supposed to encourage independence. The little people were supposed to tidy up after themselves but this way was easier. She had to restore order and fast before Magda returned. She was a teacher and Magda a lowly classroom assistant but Flora felt very inferior in her company. Magda had worked at St Mary's for years, had children of her own. She was so calm yet she could keep bums in seats. She had a voice which carried. Throughout her training Flora was repeatedly told that there was no need to shout to assert one's authority and she had been relieved since, mouse that she was, she was incapable of speaking loudly. However, now in practice, in reality, a big voice seemed very necessary, a prerequisite of the job. Magda was forever telling her what she should and shouldn't be doing. It was probably meant well but Flora often took it as criticism of her abilities. She felt belittled. The scrap of confidence that she had was shrinking. Soon it was home time. Her charges were safe and for the most-part happy. There was work to put on display. The day could therefore be considered a success. She had survived.

*

She picked up the dictionary and flicked through its leaves. Oxford English. You didn't need a dictionary in this digital age but she was an old-fashioned girl. And a bibliophile. She closed her eyes and opened the book. She set her finger down at random and opened her eyes.

"Just for fun" she explained to Tiger who was looking quizzical.

Wizen. That was the word her finger was pressed against. That was her word. It pleased her. She had always liked to think of herself as wise. But no. She squinted at the page. Oh. To wither. Dry. That didn't sound good at all. She slammed the tome shut.

"Silly game anyway."

*

She cherished these quiet moments with the newspaper. She should be doing her lesson plans or end of term reports but she was so tired and Cassie was out so she had to make the most of the opportunity. Tiger was also out so the paper was safe from attack. She snuggled into the armchair and tucked her feet up neatly underneath. Start at the back. Who has come into the world? Benjamin Arthur McGough. Rupert Montgomery Thompson-Flanders. Posh. She very much doubted he'd be one of hers in a few years time. Mia Emily Watson. She had two Mia's. Leonora Mathilde Goldstein. Nice name. Unusual without being weird. She murmured it. She used to hanker after a baby. Don't rule it out. Little Leo. She shook her head. Anyway. Who has recently left the world? Edith Anne Brennan. 96. Gone to join her husband, Magnus. Leaves behind 3 children. 7 grandchildren. 3 great grandchildren. A legacy. Much loved. Who else? Donald Dixon. 83. Reggie Yarrow. 85. Sita Kapoor. 90 Caroline Elizabeth Sophie Hall. 29. Oh no. Not much older than her. A life half-lived. Leaves behind parents. 2 brothers. Donations to B-eat. Oh how sad. She must have had an eating disorder. A girl in her year at uni had been hospitalised for anorexia. What happened to her? She couldn't even remember her name. She must ask Cassie.

*

She needed to feel better. She needed to feel more. She just needed to *feel*. It was as though Amy did all the feeling for the whole family. There was no room for anyone else's emotions. Amy took away all the joy and left them with anguish. Flora still resented her, even after all these years. How could Amy be so small yet so big? So fragile yet so powerful? Flora's nails dug into her palms. She loosened her grip. The worst thing about Amy was the confusion she caused. Nothing she did ever made any sense. Amy clearly felt a lot but what it was exactly that she felt was not clear. One had to go by her actions and try to fathom her out. She left you doubting yourself. Their parents blamed themselves. On bad days Flora thought they were right to do so. After all, they brought Amy into the Fairclough family. They were therefore responsible for the resultant unhappiness.

Maybe there weren't the words for feelings. At least none that were adequate. For example, *sad*, just didn't cut it. A tiny little word, one syllable, to represent that vastness of inner experience. We share emotions but experience them differently. She supposed. Sometimes language failed. Perhaps that explained Amy's loud silence.

*

"There's an 'ole in my bucket, dear 'Liza, dear 'Liza, there's an 'ole in my bucket, dear 'Liza, dear 'Liza, there's an…"
"What's a noll?"
"'Ole in my bucket, dear 'Liza, dear…"
"Steve, what's a noll?"
"'Liza, there's an 'ole in my bucket, dear 'Liza…"

Why had she come? What was she doing here again after all these years? She had sworn that she wouldn't do this anymore, put herself through this any longer. What had been a mild irritation was fast bubbling up inside, fast becoming rage.

"Steve! What's a noll?"
"Shurrup! Move! Bucket, dear 'Liza, dear 'Liza, there's an 'ole in my bucket…"
"Alright, let's try to keep it calm, Steve" a man intervened.
"He pushed me. Shoved me! I just want to know what a 'noll is."
"Dear 'Liza, dear, she was gettin' in my face! Let me sing my song!"
"Alright Steve, calm down. Jenny, can you give Steve some space for a bit? It's supper soon"

The man put his hand lightly against Steve's back and gently steered his singing bulk towards the men's corridor.

"Excuse me darling, do *you* know what a noll is?"

Flora flushed.

"I'm sorry"
"Why, what have you done sweetie?"
"I, um, nothing"
"Don't spend your life apologising unnecessarily. You must have low self-esteem. Are you depressed dear? Is that why they brought you in?"
"Er, no, I…"
"What's wrong with you then?"

Where should she begin? Maybe there *was* something fundamentally wrong with her.

"I'm not ill, I'm…"

"Oh no, not another one, that's terrible! They *keep* doing this, locking people up for no reason. You should write to your MP darling, that's what Sheila's doing because they've shut her away in here too and she's not mental"
"No, I'm v…"
"No, really, the government needs to know this sort of thing is going on. I saw Dr Murray this morning and I mentioned it to him but I think he's in on it too. Oh, what a to-do. Don't worry, it's supper soon"
"I'm a visitor"
"Oh, you should have said. Whose visitor? Mine? I don't know you"
"Sorry no…"
"Why, what have you done?"

Where were the nurses?

"I'm sorry that I'm not your visitor. I'm here to see Amy", Flora murmured, tired, "I think" she whispered.
"Oh. Do you know what a noll is?"
"A *hole*" Flora enunciated.

Jenny started laughing.

"Amy F or Amy P?"
"F"
"Oh"
"Do you know where she is?"
"She's got no friends. Too quiet. A *hole*! I'm so dim!" And Jenny wandered off.

The room was empty. Just tables and chairs and an abandoned game of Jenga. Amy had no friends. Why was this thought lingering in Flora's mind? This was not a surprise, not new information, the revelation of a secret. Amy had never really had friends and yes, she was very quiet. Most of the time anyway. For some reason though, hearing someone else state this made it more real, a fact in fact. It felt poignant and that was the surprising element. It hurt.

A nurse put her head around the door of the nurses' station. The staff on Maple Ward did not wear uniforms so you had to look out for the badges they wore.

"Are you alright there? Who are you here to see?"

Maybe she should ask the nurse to let her back out. She wasn't sure she was ready to speak to Amy again.

Amy has no friends though.

"Amy"
"F or P?"
"F"
"She's probably in her room. We're a bit stretched this afternoon. I can't leave the office. When someone comes along, just get them to give Amy a shout. Are you a friend?"

As opposed to foe?

"Her sister"
"Oh that's nice. Faith or Flora?"

Faith?

"Flora. There's no Faith"

The woman looked puzzled so Flora elaborated.

"I think you must be referring to Faye"

The office phone started ringing.

"Help yourself to a tea or coffee", she pointed to a small kitchen area in the corner, "Excuse me" and she ducked back inside.

Flora sat down at one of the tables. The plastic cloth was sticky so she put her hands in her lap and pushed her chair back. The radio was playing away to itself, some DJ jabbering excitedly about a competition. Something was stuck in the tread of her boot. She reached down and picked up a leaf. She was feeling a little nauseous. She tried to focus on the leaf.

It was beautiful, quivering between her thumb and index finger. It was alive in its death, flame-like in appearance. Resplendent, almost regal in its pride. Golden veins striking out, coursing over speckled scarlet. The children had a nature table set up in the classroom and it was covered in leaves but, either they were not as magnificent as this one, or she had never really paid them much heed. She had always believed that leaves were what they brought in if they couldn't find anything more interesting: a bird's nest, a shell, a mouse skull. Or maybe these were actually the more imaginative and creative children, able to see the beauty in the banal. But she would have noticed this leaf if it were amongst its counterparts, you could not fail to do so.

"Sam! Sam!"

Flora jumped.

"Saaamm!"

A young man with a red face, barely more than a boy, was thumping the window of the nurses' station. The nurse ignored him.

"Sam! He's taken my lighter! He's stolen my property!"
"I have not stolen it Robert. You know you're not allowed to have lighters in your room"

It was the calm man from earlier. The dissipator of disputes.

"Fuck off! I'm talking to Sam!"

Sam opened the door.

"Robert, will you please calm down. You are *not* to speak to staff like that. You know lighters are to be kept in the office"
"I want a smoke"

He pulled a tatty roll-up out of his pocket and put it in his mouth. The man flicked the lighter and lit the patient's cigarette.

"I think you owe Rishi an apology, Robert"

The phone started demanding Sam's attention again and she returned to her desk. Robert strode off towards the bedrooms, smoke puffing out.

"Uh, Robert. The garden please"

He pulled a face but obeyed.

"Are you okay, miss?" Rishi asked.
"Fine" Flora stuttered. These places always made her feel tense. She wanted to go home.

"Are you here to see someone?"

"Amy. Amy F"

"Well, it's your lucky day! Henry managed to coax her out. She's in the garden", he waved an arm in the direction Robert had just taken. "She might be a bit drowsy though. The early shift said they had to give her something just before we came on"

He leant into the office and picked up a clipboard before disappearing off down the female corridor.

Flora shuffled over to the window. You couldn't really call it a garden. It was a courtyard. Her gaze moved upwards and rested on the wire mesh. A cage. There was no lawn nor any flower beds, although there were some containers of soil with cigarette butts seemingly sprouting out of them. A small, sickly looking tree stood in the centre. Robert and some others were sat smoking on a picnic bench. She couldn't see Amy. She opened the window as wide as it would go, which isn't far. She needed air.

"How are you doing, Amy? You okay there?"

Another man with a clipboard was leaning against the wall, looking in Flora's direction. This must have been Henry. As she looked again, she saw that he wasn't quite watching her, but, sure enough, under Flora's window a small figure crouched.

Amy.

"Why did you have to get Amy in the first place?"
"Flora, please…"
"Well, why did we have to keep her then?"
"Flora, that's enough!"
"I hate her! She ruins everything!"

Amy had her back to Flora and was hunched over. The familiar viridescent hair was damp and tangled. It was tied up in a sort of bun on top of her head. Flora could probably count on one hand the number of times she'd seen Amy with her hair up. It was nearly always the result of their mother trying to tame it and thus, in a weird way, Amy herself. Perhaps this was what was happening here. Already pale snakes were wriggling out from the elasticated clamp though, licking the breeze for a taste of its freedom.

Amy's neck was exposed. It was deathly white and thin, a couple of bony protuberances at its base looked certain to erupt through the papery skin before Flora's very eyes. Spinous processes. It was as if one of those serpents had stretched out and bitten Flora, such was the pain that shot up to her heart and squeezed it. Tight. Amy seemed so little. Delicate. Vulnerable. Flora had never seen her this way before. This child was her big sister. Flora was frightened.

Then she noticed. Amy held a leaf in her palm. She seemed to be studying its bleached underside.

"You want to sit in the lounge and watch TV?" The clipboard man asked. "Amy?"

She did not respond but was tracing the veins with her little finger.

"Amy? You okay? What are you doing?"
"Sycamore"
"What? Come on girlie, let's go inside now. It's getting a bit nippy and you've got wet hair"

He got up and gently took Amy by the left shoulder.

"Come on", he knocked her leaf to the ground, "Supper soon", his foot shattered it.

Amy shakily rose. Her huge, globular eyes swivelled around and caught Flora in their luminous glow.

Flora dropped her head. Her leaf was a cupped hand, the five digits curling upwards, begging. Pleading.

*

When she thought of her, of Amy, something happened deep within. An anger. A rage. Bubbling up. It was Amy's fault, she was to blame. Amy did this to her, Amy had all but destroyed her, made Flora the way she was - an ineffectual being. This was what happened when you grew up in the shadow, the enormous shadow, cast by a sibling hell-bent on death. The whole family was sick. They lived in fear, they were perpetually perplexed - why? What were they doing wrong? Why wasn't their love enough? The tears that were shed, the sleepless nights. Amy was so selfish! Was she actually, genuinely suicidal? After all, this behaviour had been going on for years and Amy was very much still alive. It was hard to see it as anything more than attention-seeking. Would it ever end? Sometimes Flora hated her, really hated her. Many a time she had wished her dead but her parents would completely fall apart if this were to happen. Amy controlled everyone around her, held them hostage. She sucked the joy out of them. Amy took up so much space, not physically but emotionally. Amy was a huge presence. No one else mattered. Flora did not matter.

But every now and then, Flora would catch sight of one of the many trinkets Amy had gifted her, or an object of Amy's as innocuous as say, a toothbrush, and she would feel her heart breaking, the guilt, the pain, the sadness welling up in her chest.

*

There was a scream. Flora's heart lurched. Except it didn't. That's just the expression. It was her stomach. Vagus nerve?

"Flora! Flora! Come quick!"

She had been lying on her bed, staring at the ceiling where a dot had turned out to be a small bug. There was a substantial fissure zig-zagging across the plaster. The lampshade yellowing.

"Flora!"

From the panic in Cassie's voice, she feared what she might find. She pulled on her dressing gown.

She found Cassie in the living room. She and Tiger's gaze was fixed upward. A bird. A robin. It flew at the window repeatedly. It flapped about the light. It landed on the back of the armchair, its little breast heaving. Flora registered the terror in its eye.

"Open the window, for God's sake!"

Cassie didn't budge.

"I hate birds. They give me the creeps"

Flora pushed the glass as far as it would go.

"And I wish you wouldn't blaspheme, Flo."

The robin summoned up its strength and flew shakily out of the window. There was a streak of scarlet on the cream chair back. The robin had lost a little of its life force. Would he survive out there? Tiger was at the glass, tail twitching from side to side.

"Lily brought it in. Second one in a week."

Flora wasn't listening. She was mesmerised by the glistening globule. She touched it. Soon it would turn crusty and brown.

"Flora?"

This was the bird's essence. A little of its insides exposed. When she cut her finger the other day, as she watched the crimson trickle, she felt a tiny bit of herself had escaped, was free. She had squeezed and squeezed the wound, willing as much of herself out of the confines of her skin as possible.

"Do you think I should get a bell for her collar?"

Flora pressed hard on her scar. Nothing. The exit was sealed tight by granulation tissue. A violent image flashed through her mind. A blade slicing skin as if butter, blood spurting, pouring. Release. Escape.

*

"Flora, you're in love with places you've never been to and people you've never met."
"That's not true. What do you mean?"
"You're in a dream world. You seem to be living inside your head. I don't mean to sound harsh but you need to get in touch with reality. There's life out there."
"Cassie, that *is* a little harsh."
"Well, I can see you're not happy. You've changed, Flo."

She didn't know how to respond. Cassie was right - her life was shrinking. She lived inwardly. Get in touch with reality? If only reality could be touched. If only she had something to hold onto. Something tangible.

Cassie pulled Flora towards her. Wrapped her arms around her.

"Because I care, Flo."

That evening, when she was getting ready for bed, Flora found a note on her pillow:

Psalm 46:1 "God is our refuge and strength, an ever-present help in trouble."

*

Amy was a jumper. Flora was a teacher and Amy was a jumper. A river-jumper. Flora was very au fait with the aftermath but had only ever witnessed the one actual jump. Up until now anyway.

She must have been about four. If that. It was summer and they were staying with their grandparents. Or were they? They were in the countryside and she could picture her grandfather there but they might have rented a cottage somewhere. They used to do that sometimes. Devon, the Cotswolds, Dorset. Nana and Pops lived in Yorkshire. This didn't seem like Yorkshire. There were too many trees for it to be up on the moors.

Flora wore a *Fireman Sam* t-shirt and a pair of pink, sparkly fairy wings. She had fallen over that morning and sported a *Mr Bump* plaster on her knee. She was pushing Baby in a red and white-striped doll's pram. Baby was a blue rabbit. It was difficult to push the pram on the grass, especially at speed. Flora remembered they seemed to be in a hurry. The pram kept getting stuck in dips or tipping up. Baby fell out a couple of times.

Flora was hot. The big floppy sunhat fell over her eyes so she had to walk with her head tilted back, chin in the air, looking down her nose at where they were headed. Where were they headed? The long grass was scratchy and, at times, reached above Flora's knees. Amy was in front. She wasn't wearing any shoes. She strode on determinedly. Were those wings strapped to her back too, just visible beneath her hair? That didn't seem quite right, not for a teenager. Flora must have imagined them.

She remembered calling out, "Wait for me, Amy!" but Amy did not stop or even slow down. She merely turned her head and grinned, positively beamed, stretching out a white hand in Flora's direction. Flora recalled feeling tired and thirsty and a little bit grouchy but not scared. She trusted Amy completely. Amy adored her, doted on her, wouldn't hurt a hair on her head. Why did people say that? The most violent, dangerous criminals couldn't hurt anyone's hair because hair has no nerves and is, to all intents and purposes, dead.

A wave of sadness rolled up and over Flora's body. What happened to these two sisters? Amy loved her. That's a simple statement of fact but somehow it got lost over the years. It morphed into something else. Something far more complicated and messy. But perhaps it needn't have. Why couldn't she have just allowed it? Perhaps things would have been different if Flora had not let her heart get carried off in the confusion. Why couldn't it remain: Amy loves Flora and Flora loves Amy? Because she did, didn't she? She did love Amy. She must do or she wouldn't be hurting now.

To Flora's left had been a narrow strip of trees but it was now growing into dense woodland. The grass was less of a hindrance here, having given way to dusty earth with only small yellowy tufts to break up the brown. It was much cooler now they were in the shade. Flora was hungry. "Have you got a rumble in your tumble?" is what their mother used to ask.

"Amy, I'm hungry!" Flora called. Amy was the kind of sister that was good for buying you ice-creams or setting up spontaneous picnics, real or make-believe.

Where *were* they going? Amy was still marching, her filthy feet slapping the soil. You had to allow Amy more time than most to respond. People who didn't know her always thought she hadn't heard their enquiry so would be just starting to repeat themselves, when Amy's lips would begin to form her answer. Occasionally she would forget to add the sound to her mouth movements which could be disconcerting. She would also frequently break off mid-sentence, as if she expected you to have got the gist from the little information gleaned. She wasn't really one for words. Not one for embellishments. Her vocabulary rarely included adjectives. Or, on particularly bad days, even verbs. Flora waited.

Amy finally turned and smiled once more, holding her hand out as before, beckoning Flora to join her. Then the marching turned into bounding as she spotted some blackberries.

Flora was sitting on the parched ground, her hands stained purple. She prodded a twig down a small hole. Angry ants rose from its depths, antennae waving in protest. She wasn't scared. She giggled.

Then what? Then things get a bit jumbled in her mind. Amy said something. What had it been? What had she meant? Had she really just said "bye"? Simple as that. She was sure there had been more.

Then everything happened very fast. Amy darted off. Sounds grew louder. The birds were no longer twittering in the branches above but squawking. Suddenly the distant gentle quacking of ducks became the threatening honking of geese.

Everything went dark. There were screams. There was no splash.

No more time alone with Amy after that.

*

Flora was a teacher and Amy was a jumper and Faye was special. Faye was. Past tense.

Little Flora erased the last of Faye. Quite literally. Quite deliberately? Well, it wasn't really accidental but she could plead in a court of law that, at the tender age of six, she lacked capacity. She did know that what she was doing was wrong though. She knew she was being naughty. She remembered taking the small pad out from underneath Amy's pillow and opening it up. There on the first page was a childish and simple yet, at the same time, exquisite drawing of a tree. Not one leaf had been misplaced or forgotten. There were two little girls standing beneath it but the drawing of them was less impressive, more like one of Flora's own, with legs and arms coming straight down from the faces. No bodies.

Flora was wearing her summer uniform, a red and white gingham dress. She slipped her hand into her pocket and pulled out a garish yellow rubber. She tried it out on a bit of the tree trunk. A piece of bark. The wispy grey line vanished, never to be seen again. Just like the artist. It was too easy. A gentle press of the eraser was all it took and one by one the leaves disappeared, winter from summer.

Next the yellow obliterated one smiling, pig-tailed girl and then the other. One thing was left on the page, right at the top:

Faye.
       aye.
              ye.
                   e.

Flora looked at the page. It was covered with little black specks. Fragments of rubber. Fragments of pencil. Fragments of Faye. Flora gave a big puff and Faye blew about the bedroom. Gone.

Amy walked in just at that moment, a towel wrapped around her. She saw the now empty pad in Flora's hands.

"Oh" was all she had to say.

She pulled Flora gently onto her lap and kissed the top of her head. Opening the next page of the pad, Amy pushed Flora's finger over the white sheet. Together they traced the ghostly indentations of a beautiful tree, two little girls and a name. Faye.

*

Amy was difficult to live with. Always had been. Well, as long as Flora had known her, Amy being ten years her senior. Their parents had thought they were unable to have children and so adopted five year old Amy. Amy had been a twin. Had been or still was? Faye, her twin, had died just shortly before the adoption was finalised. Not much was known of their background. They had been found in a park as babies. No sign of the mother. Flora's parents often referred to Amy as their cabbage-patch-daughter. Amy had "behavioural difficulties" the social worker said.

*

Flora trudged through the park. She was tired. And grumpy. The children had been particularly trying today. Her backpack was heavy and her feet were sore. Her flat was the other side of the park. This may be a shortcut but the park was still vast. She used to play here as a child. A little monkey climbing trees. Tilly loved it here but they always had to keep a close eye on her because of the deer and they kept her away altogether during the rutting season when tempers and hormones went awry. Flora arrived at the lake. The water was still and glassy. It looked black today, reflecting not only the darkening sky but also her darkening humour. There was so much she needed to get done, none of which was appealing. She really didn't have time to pause here. But. But the thought of the flat and the inevitable noise and mess was not inviting. Here was peaceful. "Don't walk through the park after dark" her mother would warn. A young woman was attacked here a few years ago. It was dull. It was grey. But night had not fallen yet. There was a bench near the bank but it was broken. A sign that she should keep going. But. There was the tree. Her tree. The one she would sit under during those long summer days, devouring novel after novel. The ground was damp so she sat on a plastic bag. She lent back against the trunk, sighing as she did so. She felt the tension start to ease, her mind start to quiet. How strong, how solid her tree was. The things it must have seen. The people. Past centuries. Cassie said all living things have a soul - did that include trees? She closed her eyes and inhaled deeply. It smelt of the recent rainfall. Fresh. Earthy. The grass was long around her. She was hidden from view. But, peeping between the blades, the view was not quite hidden from her. She could make out a shadow in the distance. In the failing light it was difficult to tell if it was advancing or retreating. She didn't really care. She felt safe. She could stay here forever. This was the closest she was going to get to making time stand still, a longstanding desire of hers. As long as she didn't look at her watch she could believe that the moment was frozen. She could stay here *and* still complete all her tasks. The shadow was becoming more defined. It was a figure. Female. Flora sat forward. Something about the woman's movements looked familiar. She dug her glasses out of her bag. Yes. Yes it was. No doubt. Amy. Amy was approaching the other side of the lake, almost at a run now. Oh God. Here we go. She should intervene. But. But something stopped her. She was an observer of the scene playing out before her. She wasn't a part of it. A jogger entered stage right, a headlamp capturing her sister in its beam. For mere seconds. But long enough for Flora to see the wink and smile in her direction. And then she was gone. Swallowed by the water. The Lady of the Lake. "Shit!" The jogger's lamp scanned the surface. It was known to be deep. There were no bubbles. "Fuck!" Not even a ripple. All was still. Flora was rooted to her spot. Oddly calm.

*

She sat at a small, circular table and unpacked her rucksack. Self-conscious. How to behave? She glanced around. Young men, slicked back hair, tapped away on chrome notebooks. Yummy mummies and bonny babies. A gaggle of blonde teenaged girls slurping frappuccinos and taking selfies for Instagram. And an elderly gentleman with a neatly pressed handkerchief tucked into his breast pocket, reading *The Times*.

It was upon him that Flora's gaze lingered. His hair was a snowy white halo, framing his folded face. He wore a small pair of spectacles at the end of his nose. His collar and tie were tight and skin spilled over the top though he was by no means large. His eyes were a cloudy grey and he squinted as he read. His tweed blazer reminded her of her grandfather, now in a home with dementia. Another family member incapable at life. Another family member she ought to visit.

What was it like to be old and decrepit? To know that the end is nigh? Did things start to feel futile? It scared her when she thought about it. One's body deteriorating, features melting into each other, joints creaking.

Amy had stared death in the face a multitude of times. She wasn't afraid. She wanted to die. Why? Was life really so bad? Flora had never asked her. For as long as she could recall, Amy had been making attempts at her life. Flora had just accepted it - that was what Amy did. As she got older she became angry with her. It was so selfish. Their parents were in pieces. Their mother thought it was to do with Faye although Amy had never said as much. Twins. As if that explained everything that was odd. But why had Flora just accepted Amy's illness (if it really was an illness and not merely attention-seeking)? What did that say about her? Callous. Uncaring. Herself selfish. She remembered how she had been in awe of her big sister. Her beauty was startling. She wanted to be like her. She wanted to make someone feel the way Amy made her feel when she noticed her. All that love had turned to hate in recent years. Amy was single-handedly destroying their family.

Flora didn't want to die. It wasn't that she loved her life. She didn't. If she allowed herself to analyse it, she would realise that she was unhappy much of the time. It was this deep dejection that had led her to become the misanthrope she was today. At the grand old age of twenty-five. Now that was sad. No, she didn't want to die. She couldn't bear the thought of an eternity of nothingness. But if it truly was nothingness, she would just cease to be. She would simply stop. As the ant did when you stepped on it. But energy never ends. It has to go somewhere. It is a law of physics. Energy can neither be created nor destroyed but transforms from one form to another. Basic stuff. Was this energy the soul Cassie spoke of? Flora shook her head. That just wasn't scientific.

The elderly gentleman looked up at her from his paper. Flora flushed and sipped at her coffee. It was still too hot and burnt her tongue. She was frowning permanently these days - deep furrows had taken up residence in her young skin. She desperately wanted to ask him where he was going when he left this planet. Or was his energy going into nourishing the worms and maggots? Was that it? Suddenly a tear pricked her eyes. It took her by surprise.

*

As she was walking along, marching along, an elderly woman, all bundled up against the elements, opened her front gate and stepped out in front of Flora. She proceeded to waddle slowly, propped up by a stick, in the middle of the pavement. Flora in turn had to slow. Could this woman not have waited for her to pass? Could she not keep to one side of the pavement? Already irritable, Flora felt even more so. She was angry. Sometimes she hated people. A lot of the time. They were stupid, selfish, intensely annoying. She huffed loudly as she stepped into the road to overtake. Why was she so moody? It had quite a lot to do with the parcel she'd received that morning. Her mother had found some of her old schoolwork and thought she would like it. Didn't want it cluttering up their new house more like. Most of it had been of little interest - childish drawings, times table books. However, there was a project she'd done called *Me by Me*. She'd been awarded a merit for it. It was all about her and her family. "My best friend is Tilly". "My star sign is Taurus". "I have a big sister called Amy. She is a grown-up. She is not very well. She hurts herself. It makes my mummy sad". How could Amy do that? How could she expose a little child to her self-harm? She had stolen some of her innocence. Taken part of her childhood. It had all been about Amy. How can we help Amy? Their mother was on medication because of her. Benzos. She had become dependent.

*

The melancholy was heavy. The sadness weighed her down. Centuries of sorrowful souls clung to her. She could barely move. Her feet had turned to lead. Her head too much for her neck and shoulders to bear. Atlas carrying the weight of the world. Even her eye-lids were being dragged down. She was sinking. Sinking into the earth. Sinking deep within herself. It was so beautiful here. So peaceful. The air was still. The only sound the caw of a crow. Peaceful. And yet. What? What was this lump inside? This discomfort. An ache in the pit of her stomach. This longing. She actually needed to cry but the tear tap was off. Instead a watery mucus dripped from her nose. To lift her hand to wipe it was too effortful. She sniffed and the snort reverberated around the woods. The crow flapped ungainly away. Now she really was alone. Then it dawned on her. She was alone. She was lonely, so very lonely. And the worst of it was she had no one to tell. Her legs gave way and she dropped to her knees. She didn't try to get up. A loud sob escaped from the depths of her being. Was this how Amy felt?

*

Elision. Today's word. When talking, missing a word or syllable. Or. Merging, particularly ideas. Missing or merging. What was Flora doing?

*

It was coming more and more frequently. She could feel it now, hovering near, ready to engulf her. Again. She was two chapters into *Villette.* She placed her bookmark between the leaves and tossed the tome to one side. It would pass. She did not enjoy school holidays. She never knew what to do with herself. All this empty time. Time she feared, especially now she had this 'thing', for want of a better word. It was late morning and she was lying on top of her bed covers, still in her pyjamas. Tiger was lying stretched out long and thin beside her. He seemed to enjoy having her home. It was confusing. A lot of the time she felt empty, so much so that she sometimes questioned if she were even human. She felt like a robot, simply going through the motions of living. Lately though, when this thing came over her, she felt so full. Everything hurt. It was a blackness and weighty. It could strike at any time. When it did so she could suddenly see everything the way it really was. The truth. It made it hard to continue with the little things when she could see the futility. This time it was Charlotte Brontë who set her off. Dead. Obliterated. Nothing but these words left. No one around to remember her, no one who knew her, no one who loved her. Flora wouldn't like to be immortal but death played a lot on her mind and it frightened her. She thought of her father. All those secrets coalesced into a mass. A tumour. In his brain. She loved him so much and now he was going to leave her. It was benign and slow growing but a space-occupying lesion nevertheless. His skull didn't have space. Not for so many secrets. If only he would break his silence - his secrets were keeping him sick. Of course he denied their existence but she knew better. Even his diagnosis, his prognosis, were partial secrets. No one was to tell Amy. She was too fragile for such news. Their father. Their own dear Daddy was to join Charlotte. Was to join Faye. Wherever that was. She had a horrible, sickening feeling that it was precisely nowhere. It is a clichéd question but she asked it anyway: what was the meaning, the point of life? At least Charlotte had her words, what would be left of her dad? What indeed, would she, Flora leave? Never mind Amy, what about her? She couldn't process this classified information.

*

To think that every living thing is in a state of decay, was depressing. The only certainty in life was death. We are all dying, some, her father, faster than others. Flora was feeling despondent. Listless. When she qualified as a teacher her mother, ever the artist, had made her a beautiful card with a quotation apparently by Picasso. *The meaning of life is to find your gift. The purpose of life is to give it away*. The implication being that Flora was a gifted teacher, imparting her wisdom onto young, eager-to-learn minds. But she was not a gifted teacher. At best she was average. Mediocre. The children seemed to like her but that was probably because she was a soft touch. Discipline was not her forte. She saw herself as a failed scientist. Her degree was in biomedical science but she got a Third. Now she wasn't even a science teacher. She spent more time wiping bums and noses than imparting knowledge. It had never been her plan to teach, but she had been enthusiastic on the course, hoping she'd found her place in life. Her niche. Her parents were proud of her. But two years into the job and she was jaded.

*

It was raining. Pouring. Water cascaded out of the sky. Flora was wet through. Her hair clung to her face. Her nose dripped. It was cold and dark. She didn't have a coat, let alone an umbrella. She wanted to know what it was like, what it felt like, to be Amy. This was Amy's favourite weather. How she loved the rain. Water is essential for life to exist but Amy needed more of it than others. Flora tilted her head back, opened her mouth. She was shivering but, in a way, she was glad. Relieved. She had been trapped in the confines of her mind, pretty much dissociated from all the life around her over the last few days, and this icy wetness jolted her back. Down to Earth. Alive and a Part Of. Was this her sibling's experience? Did she struggle to escape her head?

*

The bench was too high and her legs dangled. She was a child again sitting with her daddy. She just needed an ice-cream and Tilly to complete the picture. She missed that little dog. She missed so much of those days. It was a cliché but she had been so happy and carefree. And she had felt so loved. So wanted. She looked sidelong at her father only to find he was watching her. He placed his hand on her knee.

"Talk to me"

That was not usual. Yes, she and her father spoke but never of anything of any consequence. What should she say? What did he want to talk about? He looked and sounded serious.

"Daddy, I, I…"
"It's okay you know. I'm okay."
"I wish we could turn back time"

He smiled.

"I still have time. And now I know I'm dying, I can get on with the business of living. Your mother and I are going to take a trip. We want to see the Northern Lights."

Flora wanted to ask what she was meant to do. What about her? Couldn't she come too? Who was going to look after her? But she was an adult. Independent. This was how life was meant to go. Now was her parents' time together. Time for them to enjoy life. Before it came to an end. Why did she feel abandoned?

*

Amphibious Amy. She had led a very wet life. Pluviophile. Hydrophilic. Water was tumbling from Flora's tumbler but still she did not switch off the tap. What was water? Shapeless. Formless. Tasteless. Colourless. But far from nothing. What drew Amy to it? What fuelled her obsession? The obvious thing was its might, its power to kill. Drowning was after all, Amy's modus operandi. But water could be gentle, soothing. It caressed the skin. Flora held her fingers under the stream. It was refreshing. It was cleansing. It was essential to life. Life-sustaining. Life-preserving. Perhaps she should point this out to her sister. Despite Amy's many suicide attempts she was still here. Water was deep enough to save her. Every time. Amy must know that by now. Yet she persisted. Why?

*

She thought of her mother. She longed for her mother. Not her mother the way she was now. No. The mother of her childhood. A happy mother. A mother with time. A mother able to mother. How she yearned to snuggle on the sofa with this woman. To lean into, to press against her side. So soft. The sweet scent of vanilla. The swathes of scarves enveloping her. Her mother would pull her in further, stroke her back with light fingertips, drawing circles. Her skin would tingle. Her ear against the cushioned ribcage. Slow breathing. In. Two. Three. Out. Two. Three. The heart slowly lub-dubbing as valves opened and shut. Her eyelids would grow heavy. Maybe her mother would hum softly, her voice deep, her body rumbling. Soporific. She would readjust herself. Her mother's yielding belly a pillow. Curling her fingers around the chunky beads, the ones that looked like liquorice allsorts. Love.

*

The shower was hot. Scalding. Her skin scarlet. She held out her hands, the veins bulging. Vasodilation. The fingers shrivelled like prunes and red raw around the nails from years of picking, of nibbling. She turned off the tap and stepped out of the bath. The mirror over the basin had misted up giving her a ghostly appearance. She pulled her threadbare towel around her and squatted, rocking ever so slightly back and forth on her haunches, hair dripping onto the tiles. Some guilt was appropriate, necessary even. A catalyst for change, for reparation. Excessive guilt, rumination on wrongdoings, was certain to lead to resentment and depression. She was full of resentment which in turn made her feel guilty again. Who was she?

"You've been in there a long time - are you okay?"

Her lips moved but no sound came out.

"Flora, are you in there?"
"I don't know" she murmured.

*

"Daddy! Look at me! Look what I can do!"
"That's great darling"
"You're not even looking!"
Flora hung upside down from the monkey bars, skirt over her head, spotty knickers on display. Her father tossed his paper aside and leapt as elegantly and swiftly as a gazelle over to her. He tickled her exposed stomach and she squealed. His laughter burst from his throat and he gathered her up in his arms, spinning around on the spot.

Now as she thought of her father, she thought of the mass, squeezing out his faculties. One by one. Slowly. Her dad. A good man. A gentle man. A gentleman. It just wasn't fair.

Her father sat in his armchair, cricket on the television. He pushed his glasses further up his nose. He scratched his head. Lots of hair then. His bean-pole body and limbs didn't fit the chair. He kicked off his work shoes. Little Flora sat at his feet playing with Baby, pouring tea. Her father's second toe was longer than the others and had erupted through his red sock. She had the same toes. Roman toes did he say? Or were they Greek? She reached out and touched the naked piggy. It wiggled. She looked up and he winked.

*

The mirror was to the side of her bed. She rolled over and stared into it. She couldn't catch herself blinking. She held her breath, flung her arm over the edge of the bed. This is what she'd look like dead. If she died in bed. As she probably would, the amount of time she spent there.

*

They were in a busy coffee shop.

"Right, love, I have to get going"

Her mother planted a kiss on top of her head, just like she used to. Flora wanted to pull her close. Be enveloped by the swathes of cloth. She wanted to breathe her in.

"Where are you going? Can't you stay a bit longer?"

Flora felt vulnerable. A little tearful.

"A meeting. I need a meeting, sweetheart"

Flora suddenly felt anxious.

"Are you okay, Mum?"
"Oh yes, I haven't picked up or anything like that but with everything that's going on, I need a bit of support from the rooms"

Flora's face must have given away her fear. Her alarm.

"Really, darling. It's just housekeeping for the mind. I'm an addict and always will be. But I'm a clean addict and going to meetings will help keep it that way. I'm okay, Flora"

"Can I come with you?"

Like she used to on occasion. There was something comforting about NA. Keep coming back, it works if you work it so work it, you're worth it!

"Not today, love. I need a bit of space. For me"

Her mother stroked her cheek, turned and left. She didn't look back. Flora felt rejected. Bereft. She'd had an hour of her mother's time but she wanted more. She needed more. She hadn't told her that she too was struggling. She took the last swig of her coffee, now cold. Back to the flat she supposed. She felt so alone.

*

She'd felt all this time that she'd been buried but maybe this wasn't the case. Maybe she had in fact been planted. She was where she was for a reason. She had quite deliberately been placed upon this earth. Within this life. If she could just work out this reason. If she knew why she was the way she was, perhaps life would be easier. Then again, most people bumble through life without a clue as to their purpose. At least the knowledge that there was a reason was a start. It made her feel better anyway. She patted down the soil in the window box. Enveloping the bulbs. They were not being suffocated. They were being nurtured. En-wombed not entombed. In the dark for now but bursting into the light in due course. A new beginning. That's what she had too. Now that she had an awareness.

She dropped the trowel and picked up her mobile. No messages. No surprise. If she sent Amy a text would she reply? Did she even have a number for her? What did she want to say to her anyway? Perhaps something simple - could we start again please? She was coming to realise that she still needed her big sister. She searched her contacts but Amy was not there. She must have deleted her. She called her mother.

"Mummy?" She gulped.
"Oh hi, sweetie, how are you? Everything okay?"
"I. I love you"
"I love you too, precious girl. Is everything okay?"
"Yes. Yes. Sorry. How's the new house?"
"It's fine. You don't sound yourself"
"Oh, I'm just a bit snowed under with everything. Work. You know how it is"
"Don't put so much pressure on yourself. You don't have to be perfect all the time… you hear?… Flora?"
"Do you have a number for Amy?"
"Oh. Wow. Um. No, actually. She doesn't have a phone. But you can call the ward. Do you want the number? She's not really

communicating much at the moment though. You know how she gets"
"That's why I wanted to text" She chewed her lip.
"Letter? I'm sure she'd appreciate that"
"Yes. Maybe. I'll think about it. How's Daddy?"
"He's okay, darling. He's doing well. He'd love to see you. *We'd* love to."
"I have to go now. Love you and love to Dad"
"Okay, love. Bye"

Flora sighed. A letter. Yes. Good idea. She looked up.

"Tiger! No! Off!" She clapped her hands.

Tiger dashed out of the room, kicking up soil as he leapt out of the box. A bulb lay on the floor and in its place, a turd.

*

She stared at the blank page before her, rolling her pen back and forth across it. Tabula rasa. A clean slate was what was needed. She wasn't at all sure about this. There was so much and so little to say. It all depended on how honest she was going to be but what was the point in not being honest? Should she tell Amy she loved her or hated her first? Both were true. I miss you. That was a start. Also true. I don't understand. Why are you doing this? I'm angry with you for everything you've put our family through. But I don't want to be. I want to understand. I'm ready to listen.

*

Her very existence had been inconceivable. Yet after years of trying, conceived she was. Although she always believed, misconceived. She was said to be a miracle. But that anyone exists is surely miraculous. And that people continue to exist. We are formed from next to nothing. Little more than fairy dust. Two cells, gametes, uniting, dividing, multiplying. Zygote. Embryo. Foetus. Baby. And then so utterly helpless, weak, fragile. But survive we do. Billions of us. Even those with a death wish. Amy had taught her that it's actually quite hard to die. The body always fights to live even when the mind seeks to annihilate it. This strength, this primordial drive, comes from those two cells, together containing forty-six chromosomes. It was incredible. It was bizarre. It was wondrous. She knew the biology but science was insufficient to explain what it is to be human. All these beings, no two the same, not even those genetically identical - different minds, spirits, souls. And yes, she believed in the soul. And yes, she believed in the sanctity of life. How could she not when surrounded by all these miracles? And if this life is so special, where was the celebration and the reverence? If she, Flora, were sacred, a miracle, what was she doing with herself? Where was her freedom? There were always rules, other people in charge. What gave them the right to decree how she should live her life? Was not the goal to not only survive but to be happy? Or at least content? Because she wasn't. And she didn't even seem to be headed on that path. And Amy? What life did she have locked up in institutions? Just because she didn't fit into society's norms. Her doctors were no less than agents of social control. They did it to her to keep her from harming herself but perhaps she was only driven to self-harm by the fact that she couldn't live her ideal life because of others being in control of it instead of her. But who does get to live their 'ideal' life? If she has it bad, what about child soldiers, for example? They are just being used. They are pawns. Their lives, their sacred lives, worthless. Flora felt angry. It wasn't right. This was a terrible state of affairs. There needed to be rules or there'd be anarchy, but we only get one chance at life, seemingly anyway, and many, herself included, were wasting it. Or having it wasted. She didn't want to be a teacher. She just drifted into it. She didn't want to work at all. Or at least not for anyone else. *Under* anyone else. She had to get off the conveyor belt. Out of the trap. She would help others to do the same. How exactly, she did not know. But she would start with Amy.

*

"So, have you met anyone yet? Anyone special? A nice young man?"

How she hated that question. Her mother knew not to ask but her father was persistent. Oblivious to her discomfort. She felt her face flush, her skin burning. She tugged at a loose thread on her skirt. Kehinde. Why was he in her head? There he was, sprawled across the sofa, leg hanging over its arm. Big grin. He was nice. He was a young man. What was wrong with her? She wasn't unattractive. She had never had a boyfriend. No one had ever so much as asked her out. They made comedies about virgins not much older than her. Her virginity was a source of great shame. She kept it secret. When she was about fifteen, some boys from school wolf-whistled at her and she had assumed they were poking fun at her. Kids often did back then. But maybe they did it because they actually liked her. Just maybe. What was it like to be in love? There was a whole side of being alive she was clueless about. A dimension of her self was missing. She wasn't getting the full experience of life on this earth. She was being short-changed. She watched random couples and she just couldn't understand. She knew what it was like to love a friend. Parent. Sibling. But romantic love? Her mother said she simply hadn't met the right person. Maybe she was asexual. Was that even a thing? Or was it just a word for a non-existent libido? But then there was Kenny. Again.

"Ooh, she's blushing!"
"Daddy, please!"
"Sorry, love. I'm just teasing"

He reached for his mug of tea but missed it.

"Whoops!" He laughed.

He tried again. And missed again. Flora put the cup in his hand and he shakily brought it to his lips. She couldn't watch. Instead her gaze fell upon a walking stick. This was really happening.

"Spillage in the village! Pass a tissue would you, sweetheart?"

*

How could they not tell Amy? She was going to find out sooner or later. Sooner by the looks of things. Amy would be hurt to find she'd been kept in the dark. Wouldn't that provoke a worse reaction? A more dangerous one? Flora understood her parents' decision though. The memory of Tilly's death still haunted her. A couple of hours after the news had been broken to her, Amy had been fished out of the Thames. She had jumped off Waterloo Bridge into its freezing depths. It had been January and snowing intermittently. Amy's naked body was mottled and blue. Tilly was a dog - what would Amy do if, no, when, she discovers her father is dying? Amy was in a safe place though and had a lot of support around her. Perhaps now was the best time. However, it wasn't Flora's news, her confidence, to break.

*

She looked over at Tiger sitting on her windowsill, tail twitching. He was not *just* an animal. Not a lesser being. There was a little light burning within him. He was another soul, albeit in feline form. So alive. He glanced over his shoulder at her and mewed.

"You know, don't you? You understand so much. Thank goodness I have you, my boy."

He returned to his birdwatching. A long low rumble penetrated the walls followed by a higher pitched giggle. She wanted to make herself something to eat but she didn't want to be sociable. She tiptoed over to her door and pressed her ear against it. Kehinde was simply too big for their flat. She couldn't make out what was being said. It sounded like play-fighting. She hoped that was all it was. She slowly pushed the door open and padded across the hall. She took a deep breath and held her head up high. Cassie and Kehinde were sprawled over the sofa. Her feet were in his lap and his rested on the coffee table.

"Did we wake you, Flo?"
"I wasn't asleep. It's fine"

It wasn't. It really wasn't. She couldn't breathe. There was no space. No air. Kehinde was looking up at her with those big dark eyes. Those big unfathomable eyes. Something stirred within.

"We were going to watch a movie"
"A *film*, Kenny" Cassie corrected.

His eyes were still on her, whilst his fingers played with his girlfriend's toes.

"You want to join, Flora?"

She managed a shake of the head and scurried through to the kitchen. The laughter started up again. At her expense? Paranoia. Surely. She stood staring unseeingly into the fridge. What just happened? Did Kehinde do that? Did he feel it?

"Is she alright?" She heard a deep voice inquire.

*

She was shown through a side room. "Give you more privacy". It was empty apart from three plastic covered armchairs and a bookcase with two books. 'A Tale of Two Cities'. 'A Song of Ice and Fire'. She sat on a sticky seat, shrugging off her jacket. It was stiflingly hot and stuffy but she couldn't see a radiator. Underfloor heating. She heaved the window behind her open as far as it would go, which wasn't very far. On the wall were a few posters. 'The Mental Health Act: Know Your Rights'. 'Detention Under Section 3'. Amy was on a section but Flora wasn't sure which or really what it meant other than she couldn't leave the hospital. She was uneasy, anxious even. She hadn't spoken to her sister for so long. But she was ready to talk. Ready to listen. Ready. Would Amy be willing to engage? Would she be capable? Was Flora expecting too much of her? She crossed and uncrossed her legs. The flatulent chair squeaked. They would have laughed at that once upon a time. She rested her hands in her lap. She moved them to the arms of the chair. Then back into her lap. What was taking so long? She picked at the skin around her thumb nail. She crossed her legs again. Squeak. She bounced her foot up and down. She wiggled it from side to side. The door swung open and a tall man with dishevelled hair and a pot belly stood in the entrance. He stared unblinking at Flora. She gave him a half-smile but took note of where the panic alarm was. He turned and walked off. Hurry up Amy. She looked at her watch. She couldn't stay long.

The door slowly opened and Amy slid cat-like into the room. She padded softly over to the chair nearest her sister and tucked up her slippered feet. Squeak. Her damp hair covered half her face but one haunting orb of an eye was set on Flora. She leant forward and reached out a hand to Flora's face, caressing her cheek. Amy seemed to have shrunk further since Flora's last visit. She didn't look healthy. Her skin had taken on a greyish-blue hue. It was cracked and dry, the veins prominent. Her hand was cool despite the heat. She wore an oversized brown cardigan, full of holes, over a hospital gown. Flora pitied this little big sister. There was no longer any anger. She took Amy's hand and rubbed it gently between her own. She felt huge. All this time she had afforded such power to this pathetic wastrel. She had put the disintegration of the family down to her. How could this one sick creature cause so much damage? No. It was not possible. She was no monster. She was Amy. Nothing had changed, except perhaps her physical state. She was the same person she had always been. She was the same person Flora had always loved.

Amy stopped Flora's escaping tear with her thumb. She put it to her lips, tasting its salty grief. She used to do that when Flora got upset as a child. Flora had the urge to gather her up in her arms and squeeze her so tight but something held her back. Instead she tucked Amy's hair behind her ear so she could see her whole face. Elfin. Amy smiled.

The door banged open and an elderly man came over, his grizzly face deeply lined.

"Right regular chatterbox this one" he chuckled. "Of course, back in the day, it was relatively common. Relatively common to find a body in the Thames. 'Dead houses', they had. Dotted along its banks, where they laid them out. Sad times. Hard times, to quote Dickens. And it was illegal. Suicide was a crime then. Think of the shame for the families" he tutted, shaking his head.

Who was this man? Why was he telling them this? Should she go and find a nurse?

"I'd like to be on my own with my sister, if you don't mind"
"Oh yes, understood!"

He clicked his heels together and gave a salute before exiting.

"There is no death" Amy murmured.
"Sorry?"

Amy simply smiled again. To Flora, she looked so serene, almost beatific.

"Amy" Where was she going with this? "Amy. I'm so sorry. I…" she trailed off
"You came"
"Yes, but it's been too long…"
"You came" Amy cocked her head to one side. "Before"
"I'm sorry about that. I wasn't ready. I, I couldn't do it. I've been so confused. I was angry. I'm so sorry…"

Flora dipped her head. She felt so ashamed. What kind of person abandons her sick sister?

"I'm so sorry"

Amy dug her hand into her pocket and pulled out a tiny figurine. She pressed it into Flora's palm. It was smooth and warm. Bronze. Shiny. A young girl dancing or perhaps skipping, tiny flowers in her hair. It was exquisite. Flora looked up quizzically but Amy offered no explanation.

"Supper time!" A nurse called, popping his head round the door. "Visiting time's over I'm afraid."

Flora went to give back the figure but Amy shook her head. She got up and planted a kiss on Flora's forehead.

"It's yours" she whispered.
"I'll come again. Soon. I promise."

*

Today's word was entropy. Physics. Disorder. Unpredictability. Randomness. Hmm. Interesting, quite apt. Was worse to come? Flora liked order, predictability, feeling in control, but lately this was slipping through her fingers.

*

Janus. The god of beginnings and transitions, hence January. He had two faces - was two-faced? One looking forward, the other back. That reminded her of her grandmother. She used to say she preferred sitting backwards on trains because there was more life behind her than ahead. She liked to look back, to reminisce. Flora thought that was rather morbid but her grandmother explained she always looked towards where the life was. She was always in search of life. Which direction did her father face now?

Flora wasn't sure whether something was beginning or ending. It was perhaps both. Something had left her. Something was closing. Deep within. But also, from that same place, something was springing forth, opening up, expanding. She didn't know what it was. It was as though she had awakened from a deep slumber. She could see now. The truth. Possibility. She had been in a lot of pain over what had been. She had focused on that ending. She couldn't see the new life. Not immediately. But it was growing. And as it did so she felt lighter.

*

"Why do you do it? Do you you really want to die? *Why*?

Amy shifted in her chair. A sign of discomfort? She opened her mouth but closed it again, wordless. Flora tried to read her face. Her eyes bore into Flora as if trying to communicate something, perhaps telepathically. She closed her own and tried to *feel* Amy's answer, her explanation. Nothing. She couldn't do it. And the ward was so noisy. Really though, what did she honestly expect? You are a scientist, Flora. She opened her eyes. Smiled through the frustration. The disappointment. Amy smiled in return.

"Amy, I saw you the last time. I, I think you saw me too. I want to understand."

Amy shifted in her seat once again. Drew up her knees. Hugged them. She smiled again.

"If you wanted to kill yourself, surely you would have done so by now. You keep doing the same thing over and over - are you expecting a different outcome? Because you well know that's the definition of insanity"

Amy twirled a strand of hair around her finger.

"There is no death" she whispered, almost inaudibly.
"You said that before - I don't understand. Do you mean you don't want to die?"

Silence.

"You smiled. At me. I saw."

Amy grasped Flora's hand, stroked the back.

"You *do* understand… All that matters… You know."

The tiny person winked. Perhaps. Then before Flora's very eyes the shimmering bronze melted away revealing a mass of dark curls crowned with a wreath of white blossom and ivy leaves. She wore a forest-green slip and her skin was tanned with a smattering of freckles across her nose. She had a mischievous grin playing about her lips. She stretched her arms as if awakening from a long, deep slumber, and pointed the toes of each little foot in turn before skipping daintily off her plinth and twirling across the coffee table towards Flora. The laughter that bubbled up from her person was almost musical. She then sat on the edge of the table, swinging her legs prettily. Flora rubbed her eyes. She had been working too hard. She had fallen asleep. This was a dream.

When she reopened her eyes she found this beautiful creature sitting next to her on the sofa. She was now the size of a young child. Tiger was curled up in her lap, purring, as she sat cross-legged. Flora let out an involuntary gasp. She had to pinch herself and shook her head in disbelief. The girl merely smiled and giggled again. She leant towards Flora and clasped her hand. The pudgy fingers were soft and warm to the touch. This was no dream. Cassie's music could be heard thud-thudding beyond her bedroom door. The smell of fresh coffee wafted through from the kitchen. A car honked its horn on the busy road outside. The net curtain flapped gently in the breeze.

"Who…?" Flora managed. She was trembling.
"You know who I am."
"I. I don't understand" she stammered.
"Ab aeturnum." The child paused. When Flora didn't respond she continued, "From the beginning of time." Another pause. For effect? Was this imp deliberately being cryptic? "You know me. It's your own sister. It's Faye."

The little girl had turned serious. Her eyes grew wide. Her mouth formed a perfect pout. Tiger stretched out and yawned, revealing needle-like incisors, before jumping down and sashaying towards the door.

Flora was incredulous. The child. Faye. Faye's eyes misted over, tears welling up. She sniffed and dragged her arm across her nose.

"Flora!" Cassie called, stomping into the room in her Dr Martins. "Are you all right? You look like you've seen a ghost." She looked concerned. "What's this?" She picked up the little bronze figure from the table.

*

There was something unsatisfying about Flora's relationships. Most of the people in her life were children and, let's face it, children were far from satisfactory. But that was okay. That was to be expected. They were not yet fully formed, fully themselves. Their minds were plastic. Malleable. They hadn't been around long enough to have any depth to them. At least there was potential though. But Cassie, for example. They spoke a different language. Flora tried so hard to relate to her but simply couldn't. And Cassie certainly didn't understand Flora. Flora wanted more. She wanted more from everybody. She was greedy. Nobody was enough. Enough to satisfy her craving. But a craving for what exactly? Connection. Deep connection. A merging of minds. Of souls. She wanted to have animated exchanges of ideas, concepts. She wanted to explore her own mind by opening it up to another. She wanted someone to laugh with. She wanted someone to cry with. She felt almost desperate. There was so much in her head. In her heart. She wanted to turn herself inside out sometimes so someone else could see and understand and then that someone would turn himself, herself, inside out for her. Quiet Amy. Absent Amy. Could she be Flora's someone? Her soul sister if not her blood sister. Amy hardly said a word but maybe that was because she, like Flora, was without a someone. A someone to bare her soul to. Was there anyone strong enough to bear such a soul though? Amy's mind was sick and broken after all. Who knows what darkness lay within her grey matter?

*

"Cass, can I ask you something?"

Cassie was sprawled on the floor surrounded by exercise books. Year 5 maths homework. She taught at St Winnifred's, a private girls' school. She was working her way through a packet of digestives. Flora stared at the crumbs.

"I can't work out what this kid is doing. I keep telling them to show their working and she sort of has but, it's bizarre, I don't get it…"

Flora sat up.

"Let's see"

She looked at the rows of neat numbers, no crossings out. She tried to take in the information but the calculations swam about on the page. She furrowed her brow. Tried to look like she was concentrating.

"See what I mean? I'm going to have to speak to her, go over it again"

There was a soap on the television, the sound turned right down. Cassie always worked in front of some soap or other. She watched them all.

"Anyway, what did you want to ask me? Did you get your numeracy planning done?"
"Hmm? Oh yeah. Done."

A man on the screen was crying into his whisky. He had a black eye. A young blonde woman with smudged mascara was shouting at him. She threw a framed photograph across the room.

"Ooh, turn the sound up, quick! Kim's onto him!"

Cassie looked gleeful.

"Cassie"
"Oh. Sorry, Flo. You have my full attention. Promise"
"Um, how do you feel, Cass?"

She laughed.

"What? I'm fine, just behind on my marking!"
"No, I mean, in life, generally. What's your experience? Emotionally speaking"

The couple on the TV were emoting all over the place. Was that what people did?

"Where's this coming from?"

"I'm curious, that's all. We talk about what's happening externally and you always look chilled, happy, I just wondered what's inside?"
"Okay. Um. I'm okay inside. Fine. I don't really think about it"
"Fine isn't an emotion"
"You sound like a shrink! Why, how do you feel?"
"I. I. Don't know. Not exactly. I feel a lot. Maybe too much at times. More than I used to. I think. I don't know"

Cassie laughed.

"You're an odd-bod, Flo!"

Flora forced a smile.

"I feel good, Flo. I'm happy, positive, upbeat. What you see is what you get with me. Are you alright?"
"Yes, I'm fine. You're right - I'm a bit odd!"

They turned to face the screen simultaneously. The credits were rolling. There was a helpline to call if you'd been affected by any of the issues in the programme. Some people's lives must really be that dramatic.

"You want a cuppa?"
"But you must struggle sometimes?"
"Yeah, getting ready for parents evenings!"

Was her friend deliberately evasive or was she generally unable to look internally and find the words? Was she emotionally unintelligent? Was that it?

Cassie must have seen Flora was serious.

"Of course I do. I'm human, we all do! But I hand it over. To God. Wait there!"

She ran out of the room then bounced back in, book in hand.

"This is my bible. I write my prayers in the margins with the date. At the end of the year I go back through it and tick the ones that have been answered"

Flora sighed, her face blank. Why must everything go back to that book?

"A lot of the prayers are my struggles"
"Your feelings?"
"Um, I guess. My problems. Which affect my feelings. I always feel better when I pray. Like a load has been lifted"
"I'll put the kettle on"

*

"Flora, it's okay. It wasn't you. You don't have to keep blaming yourself."

Flora jerked upright in bed. It was dark. Her eyes took a while to adjust to the gloom. That's what comes of having cones as well as rods in the human eye. Tiger would have no such trouble. What a vivid dream! She reached for her phone. 3am. The witching hour. She needed to pee.

When she returned to her room the light was on. Odd. She had deliberately left it off to avoid its harsh glare. It was the child. It was Faye. She sat hugging her knees on the end of the bed. Sucking her thumb. Not again. The little girl patted the duvet beside her and Flora sat obediently. No giggles this time.

"It wasn't you" the child lisped. "I died before you were born. Before you were conceived. So it can't have been you."

Flora could not speak. No one spoke of Faye's death. She didn't know what happened. Faye placed her cool little hand on Flora's. Flora was very aware it had been in her mouth and twitched uncomfortably. Faye continued earnestly.

"It was your dad."

This provoked a response.

"It can't have been! He never even met you!"
"He did. He met a part of me. He met my source. I was a part of this family before I was even considered."
"You're not making any sense. Dad's no killer!"

She was getting cross. She had enough trouble with impudent infants during the day and now there was one haunting her nights.

"Oh no, he didn't kill me! He took my life. There's a difference."

44

"Oh for goodness sake. I'm going to get a glass of water and when I get back you'll be gone."

She marched into the kitchen. There were no clean glasses. She grabbed a mug instead. She didn't want to return to the bedroom. Tiger circled her legs, mewing.

"It's not breakfast time" she hissed, but poured some biscuits into his bowl anyway.

She shuffled into the sitting room. Where was that figurine? She was sure she'd left it on the mantel piece. Cassie must have moved it. It was a bit chilly and her skin prickled. The flat was silent but for the hum of the fridge and the crunching of kibble. She rubbed her arms and inhaled deeply. This was ridiculous. She marched back to her room. Dark once more. There didn't seem to be any child. She flopped into bed and pulled the covers up over her head. Something moved by her feet. Tiger.

"Flora" came a little whisper.
"I don't believe in ghosts!" She snapped, keeping her eyes tight shut.
"I'm no ghost", she sounded indignant. "I'm your sister. I'm Faye."

If she ignored her maybe she'd leave her alone. She had to be up at six. She must get to sleep. Faye wasn't her sister. Never had been. They never met. They shared no DNA. Faye was Amy's past life. Her backstory.

"Speak to Amy. She knows. She knows the truth."

Flora pretended not to hear.

*

What did Faye mean? Her father took her life? She just couldn't imagine it. She needed to know more about these sisters. About *her* sisters. Her family. Daddy, did you kill Faye? No. She couldn't. The very notion was preposterous. He'd laugh. And then when he saw she was serious, he'd be deeply wounded. Faye had told her to talk to Amy. Well. Yes. That she could do. Amy wouldn't judge her for it. She felt sure of that. After all, this whole situation had arisen since Amy gave her that figurine. A tapping interrupted her train of thought. She tried to ignore it but it was quite insistent. Tap. Tap. Tap. Soft at first but growing louder now, more demanding of her attention. Morse code. Dot. Dot. Dot. Dash. Dash. Dot. Dot. Dot. SOS. She followed Tiger's gaze upwards. A moth. That's all. Repeatedly fluttering into the light, believing there was something beyond it. Something more. Icarus flying too close to the sun. Anyway. Ignore it. Not everything has to mean something. Does it? She would talk to Amy. And maybe her parents. For a backstory. Of course her father wasn't a murderer or a taker-of-lives, if that's how you want to put it. Ridiculous. The whole thing was crazy. She hadn't been sleeping well. She had too much work to do. She was worried about losing her dad. Stress. That's what this was. Faye was a very vivid figment of her overactive imagination. Her mind trying to fill the gaps in the story. Tap. Tap. The moth dropped onto the carpet beside her. Twitch. Twitch. Gone.

*

The woman's hair was slicked back. Black lacquer. Her skin was white but not the translucent white of Amy's. White emulsion. She wore heavy eye make-up and her thin lips were dark. She kept bringing her hand up to them as if trying to prevent something from slipping out. Venom perhaps, Flora pondered. No. She shouldn't judge. She looked down at her list. Phoenix's mother. Mrs Moore.

"Well?"

Flora coughed.

"I'm sorry. Mrs Moore. I'm Miss Fairclough - Flora. I'm Phoenix's teacher."
"I'm not Mrs Moore for starters - I'm Mrs Hetherington, Phoenix's grandmother"
"Oh, I do beg your pardon, it's just you don't look old enough"

The already narrow eyes, narrowed further.

"Meaning?"

Flora shifted uncomfortably in her seat. She felt her temperature rise.

"Um, nothing. It, it was a compliment"

Mrs Hetherington was glaring at her. They were so close Flora could see the powder on her face, could smell the nicotine on her breath and the notes of mint trying to mask it. The woman hardly blinked. She refused to drop her gaze. Flora dropped hers to the file before her. Phoenix Moore. Her mouth was dry. She slipped a hand into her pocket. It was still there. The key. Another gift from Amy. My life in a hundred objects. It was a fairly ordinary looking key. Not a rusty old iron one. That would have been intriguing. Exciting even. Not a little sharp key to a diary. How she would love to read Amy's innermost thoughts. No. Just a smallish silver affair. The key to a padlock perhaps? What did Amy want her to unlock? To discover?

"So, what can you tell me about my grandson?"

The Phoenix rises from the ashes.

*

Flora always felt so self-conscious. Her limbs would go rigid. Wooden. They wouldn't do what she wanted. What she pictured in her mind. She loved music. She could feel its beat. The rhythm. The natural thing would then be to express how it made her feel. To become a part of the melody. Her mother had recently taken up biodanza. The dance of life. "I lose myself in the music". She was not self-conscious. Awkward. Flora envied her ease of expression. The children were all comfortable with leaping, twirling and swirling, contorting their supple little bodies into a variety of shapes. There was something innate, something primal about dance.

She wandered into the living room and turned on the radio. Cassie was out. No one was looking. She closed the curtains just in case. Stravinsky. She knew the piece well. She turned the volume up and closed her eyes. Let go. Just let go. She was down on the floor. She was reaching high in the air. She was stomping her feet. She visualised the notes leaping from the stave and carrying her away with them.

*

"I found this key earlier - Cassie didn't recognise it. Any clue?"

A clue was just what she needed. Kehinde kept tossing it up in the air. This grated on Flora. She felt protective of her key. She felt it was fragile. And almost sacred. She had built it up in her mind to be of huge significance, of great importance. Her sister had entrusted her with it. And the treasure it was to reveal to her.

"It's mine"

She held out her hand ready to catch but Kehinde held onto it.

"What's it worth?" He grinned.

Where was Cassie?

"Very funny"
"Okay, which hand?"

He held out two clenched fists. Flora pointed to the left one. He slowly uncurled his fingers, chuckling. There it lay.

"Okay, okay, you win. Here's your key"

He placed it gently in Flora's palm, his own hand lingering. Her skin scorched by his fingers. *And palm to palm is holy palmers' kiss.* She slipped the key into her pocket and shook her scalded hand. He laughed and turned the television on.

*

The air was thick, laden with moisture from the night's rainfall. There had been a storm. She and Tilly had lain awake under the covers, her eyes heavy with sleep, Tilly's wide as saucers. The rain slashed the window pane, the glass rattling in its timber. The wind slipped in through the cracks and wolf-whistled, the mildewed curtain billowed. Her papers were tossed across the room. God snapped a shot with His flash and the thunder boomed shortly after. Tilly whimpered, pawing at her arm. She stroked her curly coat. She reminded Flora of a little lamb. It was all over by 3am.

Such rage. Such violence. And now peace. The only sounds were the caw of a solitary crow and the crackle of the frozen bracken underfoot. Was it a crow or a raven? If there is one, it's a crow, if a flock, it's ravens - was that the right way round? The mist

48

deadened all sound, viscous like treacle it was. It swirled slowly between the skeleton trees. The sun hid behind the cloud. At least, one assumed it was there. A rabbit darted out ahead and scuttled away, swallowed by the mirk. Tilly dashed after it, her ears flopping up and down as she leapt through the undergrowth. She too was gobbled up. Phagocytosed. She should have been studying. What was she doing here in this grim northern land?

The gale was now a gentle breeze. It licked at Flora's face, tussling her hair. Shadows of the past moved all around. Imprints of long lost friends. History engulfed her.

As her mind pondered this fact, she tripped on a tree root and fell. She lay still on the cold, moist earth. She rolled over, leaf litter sticking to her coat, and looked up at the branches. A squirrel. Family *Sciuridae*. Why did she know that? A tear rolled down her cheek. Just one. Life pressed down on her, stamped on her chest, crushing her ribs and the lungs they enclosed. She couldn't get up. She was weighed down. Another tear. She tasted its warm saltiness. Her shallow breath was ragged. Or was it death? Always there. Lingering. For someone so young she spent an awful lot of time looking behind her. What had been before. Who. For someone so young there was a lot behind her. There were many. Right now they were on top of her. They seeped into the pores of her skin. Into her very being. Osmosis. Deep inside, life and death merged. Limbo. How to get past this? How to move on? Which way was forward?

A bark exploded into the woods like a rifle shot. Tilly. Flora's eyes snapped open. Awake. Alive. She leapt to her feet, spinning around and stumbling over the uneven ground. A second shot. She flew. Something was not right. Her shoe came off. A ballet pump. Completely impractical for such a terrain. She lurched, ricocheting from one tree to the next, the rough bark grazing her hands. Hands already raw with chilblains. The mist oozed over her. "Tilly!" She screamed. Suddenly there the little dog was. Her fur stood on end, her tail beating in a circular motion. Flora followed the direction of her gaze. At the base of an old, decaying tree, strangled by ivy, was a small mound. A small grey boulder. It too was covered by ivy. She approached gingerly.

It wasn't a boulder. Tilly squeaked. It was a mouldy twill blanket, completely sodden. Flora pulled back the vines and tentatively lifted it to reveal a pair of little white patent leather shoes.

Impossibly white. Not a speck of dirt on them. Tilly sniffed from a safe distance. Flora hauled the rest of the blanket up and threw it aside. A tiny sleeping child, curled tight in a ball, thumb in her mouth. All colour seemed to have drained from her. She wore nothing but the shoes and what looked like a lace petticoat. Again, impossibly white. Her skin was porcelain but for a blueish hue to the lips, finger tips and eyelids. And a spray of dainty blue freckles across her nose. Her hair was fine and wispy, so pale in colour that it blended with her skin. A little girl made of ice. So exquisitely detailed. Tucked behind her ear was a sprig of cherry blossom. Incongruous with the season.

Flora reached out her hand to stroke her back, to wake her from her slumber. Despite the sopping wet blanket she was bone dry. She did not stir and the mist rolled around them. Time was passing and still it did not lift. If anything it was growing denser. A shiver jerked through Flora. Fear.

An almighty CRACK! Followed swiftly by a bark. A branch of the ancient tree crashed to the ground beside her, narrowly missing Tilly. When she looked back to check the child, she had vanished. Leaning against the trunk was a small stone cross. Before it, the blossom.

And then it dawned on her. Realisation flowed through her veins. Nausea at the back of her throat. She understood. Long gone but not forgotten, try as she might. Not forgotten. Colder than the clay above her. But very much with Flora.

She woke up with a gasp. Her pyjamas were damp. Her hair stuck to her forehead. It was still dark. Tiger repositioned himself at her feet. She shivered. There was a heaviness, an ache, in the pit of her stomach. It hadn't been a dream. It was more than that. It had to be. She had travelled to a different realm. Beyond the earth, beyond the dream world, perhaps that plane between life and death. If there was a heaven, this place was on the way. This northern wood. Her beloved Tilly. The girl. The heaviness was spreading. She was made of lead. She curled up in a tight ball. A foetus. Everything hurt.

*

"Everybody, eyes to the front, fingers on lips"

Flora clapped her hands.

"Turn on those listening ears"

She felt close to tears. She felt like walking out.

"Uh, Miss Fairclough has asked you to stop what you're doing and listen!"

The children fell silent. Flora smiled weakly at Magda.

There was a hand up at the back of the classroom, waving frantically.

"Yes? What's the matter?"

The little girl stood up. She walked slowly towards the front. *Here? Really?*

"Speak to Amy" she lisped.

"Flora? Are you okay?"

Thirty pairs of eyes were upon her. Faye had vanished.

"I. I. I need some air. Can you take over?"

Flora fled the scene.

*

The wind was biting. It blasted against her relentlessly. She couldn't get a breath in so forceful was it against her face. Her eyes stung. It was as if the wind didn't want her to get to where she wanted to go. It kept knocking her back. But she wasn't even sure where she was going. She just had to get out. In her mind she was on a quest for answers. A fact finding mission. Who was Amy? Really, who was this sister of hers? And Faye? Realistically though, where could she find these answers? She stopped abruptly. Looked up. She had walked quite a way without noticing. She wasn't even sure exactly where she was. She rummaged through her bag for her phone. Her parents were keeping things from her. She tucked herself into a bus shelter. Dialled the number.

"Flora? Everything okay, love?"

She put her finger in one ear as she strained to hear past the gale.

"What happened to Faye?"
"What?"
"What happened to Faye?"
"Yes, I heard, you just took me by surprise"
"Well?"
"She died. She had an undiagnosed heart condition, you know this"
"Prolonged QT syndrome, yes, I know"
"What's all this about then, lovely?"
"I. I. I don't know. I'm just trying to piece things together in my mind. Something I heard."
"It was over thirty years ago"

Neither spoke.

"Flora? You still there?"
"Yes"
"Are you okay? You don't seem yourself"
"Where were you when she died?"
"Oh gosh. It's a bit sad. We were getting the house ready for her and Amy when we got the call. I was decorating her room. A Little Mermaid mural. She loved Disney. Such a sweet little soul she was. We were so excited. Your father was doing the garden. Making it more child-friendly. He was putting up the swing. Had to lose a couple of trees. Oh, it was a horrible, horrible shock. We loved her already. And of course we worried for Amy."

Flora noted the pain in her mother's voice.

"Sorry Mum"
"It's okay, sweetheart. Still hurts but that's natural. As far as I was concerned I was her mother, you know?"
"What about the birth family?"
"Well, they were never traced. I wish we knew more about them. I'm sure it's been hard for Amy not knowing where she came from. We knew so little about our girls. Me and your dad, we wanted them so much, we've tried our hardest to convey this to your sister

but I don't think she can shake off the fact that her biological mother didn't want her. And you know of course that part of her BPD is a huge fear of abandonment. It all makes sense, hey?"
"Hmm. Yes. It all makes sense"
"What did you hear?"
"What?"
"You said you heard something"
"Oh something and nothing. Nothing. I have to go. I love you, Mummy"
"Oh. Okay, I love you t-"

Flora hung up. Yes. It all made sense.

*

They were praying for her. For *her*. She didn't feel anything. Well, she felt awkward. That was an understatement. But she didn't feel the earth move beneath her. She didn't feel the heavens open up above her. There was no host of golden angels singing Hallelujah. This praying wasn't at all what she expected when Cassie asked if she and Kehinde could do it. If she'd known this was coming she would never have agreed. In fact she only consented to get Cassie off her case. They were sitting on the sofa, the three of them, Kehinde taking an arm as it was only a little two-seater. Cassie had a hand on her shoulder, Kehinde on her upper back, heads bowed solemnly. This wasn't a quiet clasped hands affair. Oh no. Cassie was most vociferous. This was an impassioned plea. Every time she thought it was over there was more. They were on a mission to save her soul.

"We ask you, Lord, to come unto our sister, Flora, to enter her..."

She didn't like the sound of that. Her mind wandered, their words became background. Kehinde was wearing a particularly potent aftershave. She could almost taste it. The chemicals caught in her throat and she tried not to cough. She kept swallowing and her eyes smarted. She tried to distract herself from the tickle. Kehinde's Adam's apple, his thyroid cartilage, bobbed up and down. There was movement behind his eyelids. His lips were ever so slightly parted. What was it like to be kissed? What did Kehinde taste like? She scanned his body. He was beautiful. She allowed herself the thought.

"...may she experience the ultimate, perfect love, the love that comes from a relationship with Christ..."

*

The room was very neat and spotlessly clean. Sunlight poured through the window. The walls were painted lilac and there was a lilac and cream striped roller blind and matching bed covers. A sheepskin rug covered the laminate flooring. There was a desk, a wardrobe and not much else. It was not how Flora imagined her sister's room would be. It looked clinical.

"I'll leave you to it then"

That was Amy's key worker at Beaumont House. Amy had given Flora consent to be in her room whilst she was in hospital. Amy lived in a 'supported' house because their parents couldn't cope with her at home and she wasn't safe to live independently. Amy had been here for almost two years now but the support still wasn't enough to stop the cycle of hospital admissions. Sadly.

Flora thought there would be more *Amy* present in the room. She thought she might learn something about her sister. She hoped. There were several teddies on the bed, most of which she recognised from childhood. She picked up Henry Bear and moved over to the desk, breathing in his mustiness. He'd lost an eye since she last saw him. There was nothing on the desk but a pot of pens. She opened the top drawer. Staring up at her was her six year old self, gappy teeth and glasses. Underneath were some black and white shots of people she didn't know, lots of trees, flowers, nature. There was Tilly. The photos were good. Artistic. Since when was Amy into photography? She replaced the pictures and slid open the next drawer. There was a box and an envelope with her name on it in beautiful calligraphy. She picked it up. It had not been sealed shut. It was addressed to her, she could open it surely? This was it. Here lay what she was looking for. Answers. Meaning. She felt her heart quicken. Her hands were shaking. This was what Amy wanted for her to find by inviting her here. The envelope held a short note.

Dearest Flora,
        I miss you so much. How I wish I could make you understand. I love you. You are my everything - always have been, from the day you were born. Did you know I chose your name? My

little May-flower. You are the eternal Spring. We may not be of the same blood but we have something far deeper that binds us together - we are *ad idem*, of the same mind. We are kindred spirits. We are a trio - you, me and darling Faye, a triumvirate. Let me tell you about Faye

And that was where it ended. Flora flipped the page over. It was blank. Amy didn't finish. What about Faye? Wow. She half sat, half collapsed on the floor. The sun had disappeared behind a cloud and the room grew dark. She shuddered. It was suddenly cold. She could hardly believe that Amy had penned the letter. Was it possible for Amy to be so loquacious? So eloquent? What was a triumvirate? Could she keep the page? Was it hers now? Then she remembered the box. She reached into the drawer and pulled it out. It was light. It felt empty. A wooden casket, its lid carved with Celtic knots. Pretty. She couldn't open it. It was locked. The key. She had it on a cord round her neck. Yes. At last. It fitted the lock and turned easily. She took a breath and opened it. Oh. What did it mean? It had to mean something. There was a twig and a dried up, brittle old leaf. It disintegrated in her fingers and she felt guilty. A little bronze figure lay at the bottom. It was identical to hers. A young girl skipping. A pressed flower - a cherry blossom. Then a passport-sized photo. It wasn't very sharp but it didn't need to be. The girl. The child. Faye. The same dark curls and up-turned nose. Her head couldn't take it all in.

*

In she marched. Along with a hundred others. The British Museum. The central court was light and airy despite the crowds. She turned around and around. She felt dizzy. Which way? The Romans in Britain. That was what she needed. She felt the small bulge in her coat pocket and patted it. Smiled. Here she felt sure lay answers.

On her way she passed a throng of people, buzzing around a cabinet like wasps about a jar of spilled jam. Her time was limited but her curiosity was aroused. What were they looking at? She didn't want to join them as there was the distinct possibility of being crushed. Besides, she was not entirely sure how exactly she could join in even if she wanted to. A human wall had formed, several bodies deep. She would wait her turn. It never came. The larger the mob grew, the more people were attracted to it. This made little sense to Flora: the larger a crowd, the further away she wanted to be. As she stood musing on this observation, she suddenly became aware that the gathering had grown sufficiently to have engulfed her. She had entered the swarm unwittingly and thus become a tourist.

A cacophony of languages, none of which she was able to distinguish. Phone cameras thrust forwards and upwards. Pushing. Shoving. Jostling for prime position. A constant force from behind pushing her onwards even though there was nowhere to go but into those in front. Condensation formed on the glass. Sticky fingers smeared it. Finally she got a glimpse of the relic causing all the excitement. The Rosetta Stone. It was smaller than she had imagined. There was a notice explaining the significance of this ancient, inscribed lump of rock but she needed air and didn't fancy her chances of getting to the information and then maintaining her standpoint for sufficient time to read and digest the facts. She crouched down and, unable to turn around, wriggled backwards and out. Free.

The section she required was much less congested, quieter, civilised. She could breathe again. She peered into a cabinet. Coins. Think of all the palms they had laid upon, all the purses they had rattled inside. She desperately wanted to hold one. To connect with another from a different age. With one touch she could wipe away the centuries. She placed her hand on the glass. As close as she was going to get. Imagine being a curator in a place like this. She would love that. She could live and breathe history.

She shuffled along. A tag from a dog's collar. *"Hold me lest I flee and return me to my master, Viventius on the estate of Callistus."* This is what Tilly would have worn a couple of thousand years ago. She felt the humanity. Years passed but people were essentially the same. Denchers made of gold and bone. Beautiful jewellery that could be contemporary. An invitation from a woman, Claudia Severa, inviting her sister, Lepidina to her birthday party. Both long gone but her words remain inscribed on that ancient wood. It seems we are always leaving bits of ourselves behind. Echoes.

And then, there it was. Flora gave a sharp intake of breath. She pressed her face up against the glass. A little figure not dissimilar to the one in her pocket. It looked of great age being markedly corroded with both a hand and foot missing. She brought out her own. It glinted in the bright light of the gallery. It looked brand new. A *lar* apparently. A Roman protective spirit. She read on: *"The term is used particularly for ancestral gods of a Roman household (lares familiares)."*

*

Her lar was a link to Amy. A bridge between two souls. The connection she had yearned for. Her inner world and Amy's were spinning their separate ways. Unknown entities to each other. Unexplored territories. Usually words would form the link. Bridge the gap. But Amy was anything but usual. The lar was her way of communicating. Her way of connecting. And the lar, the portal between these two sisters? A third sister. Flora liked that. It was neat. She was not alone. Never had been.

*

How her brain ached. Thinking. Thinking. All night. She had not slept. Her body was tired but her mind was busy. She'd gone through the usual routine - shower, read in bed, light out shortly before midnight - but she couldn't get comfortable, was first too hot, then too cold, tossing and turning. Tiger quickly gave up being her bed-buddy and curled up on the rug on the floor. Ideas kept coming to her and, at the time anyway, felt groundbreaking and she yearned to share them with someone. As there was no one, at around 2.30am she gave up trying to sleep, turned the light on and started scribbling away. Was she the only person to ever think this way? Was she the only person able to *feel* at this level, this depth? When she thought of the billions of people in the world, and the millennia that people have existed, it seemed unlikely. But then again, there had never been another Flora Fairclough with her exact genetic make-up. And there would never be another. She was unique. So, could the workings, the musings, of her mind be also? She'd never had great self-esteem and she knew she was no genius but she was coming to believe that maybe, just maybe, she had this life sussed. The fundamentals anyway. Not an intellectual genius but perhaps she possessed an emotional sagacity. Was this a grandiose belief? It was as though she had inverted herself during the night, looked in the mirror, seen, and understood herself. And, she felt, that to do so, was to have understanding of everything, for the self was surely all. You could never fully comprehend something beyond your sphere of self, another human. Not fully. She had, in a way therefore, been to the limits of the universe. Could there be another person in possession of equal perspicacity of consciousness for her to share her mind? Or was she destined to fly solo with her knowledge?

But perhaps Amy shared her profundity of feeling. Doctors explained that another name for BPD was Emotionally Unstable Personality Disorder. Amy had difficulty regulating her emotions. She couldn't cope with the emotions she experienced. The patterns of behaviour seen in the disorder can come about after childhood neglect or trauma. So, Flora took this to mean that Amy *felt* life more than the average person. But unstable? Amy always seemed so calm, so peaceful, no matter what she had just done to herself. She never looked to be in turmoil. In fact, had Flora ever seen her cry? It seemed to her that her sister was very much in control of her emotions. Or at least at hiding or masking them. What was it that Amy had said to her? *All that matters, you know.* Amy could see inside her. She recognised a fellow master of internal landscapes. Flora knew and understood everything that was of any true importance. And Amy's actions weren't erratic, 'unstable'. Not if you thought about it. Her behaviour had become quite predictable over the years. If she wasn't in hospital, you knew it wouldn't be long before she was being dragged from some body of water or other. That's how it was. To Flora, Amy was one of the most stable, consistent people in her life.

*

But still there was Faye. Flora was on the cusp of realisation. She was so close. What did she know for certain? Faye was dead. Sort of. Her father, if he didn't kill her, was somehow implicated. Maybe. Faye was represented by a lar. To be worshipped by Flora. Presumably. At the time of Faye's death, her father was working in the garden. Chopping down trees. He killed the trees in doing so. In her dream, Faye was found connected with a tree. In Amy's box there had been a leaf, a flower, a photograph. Faye's life was dependent on trees? On a particular tree? The one destroyed by her father? Yes! That made sense, that was it! It had to be. That's what Amy was trying to tell her. Faye was some kind of tree spirit. What were they called? She grabbed her phone. Faye was a dryad! She read on… *can be killed by the destruction of their tree.* In mythology. And myth was a story or false belief. This was real though. And at one time these dryads were semi-deities. People believed in them. They were not always mythical. Just because

Jesus came along, it didn't mean that these ancient gods disappeared! They walk among us. Here. Now.

*

"Amy! Amy! I get it!"

Amy shuffled into the little room. The same one as before.

"I'll leave you to it", the nurse closed the door.

Amy looked a little puzzled. She approached Flora slowly. She seemed to have shrunk further still, her face gaunt. Flora grabbed her and squeezed her tight. She didn't want to let go. Not now. Not ever.

"Flora"

Flora inhaled her sister's sweet scent. Baby powder.

"Flora"

Amy pulled away, plopped down into the chair, patting the one next to it. Flora sat.

"I've been researching"

She stood again. Knelt at Amy's feet. Grasped her hands.

"All this time you've been telling me and I haven't been listening"

Amy cocked her head.

"About Faye! About what she was. She was a dryad wasn't she!"

Amy stroked Flora's hair, tucked it behind her ear.

"And you, her twin, I know what you are - you're a water nymph, a naiad! Everything makes sense now - there's nothing wrong with you, you're not suicidal, you need water to live! I get it! I get you, Amy!"

Amy started to laugh. Not her usual quiet giggle but a roar from deep within, head thrown back. Flora joined her. She laughed until the tears came and her ribs ached. This was joy. Elation. Flora wanted to bottle the happiness to keep it forever.

"And you" Amy gasped. "Ad idem".

*

She felt full to bursting. She could explode. She couldn't sit still. She had the flat to herself - even Tiger was out. It was silent but for the hum of the fridge and the distant squawk of a small baby. Neighbours she had never even nodded to, let alone said hello. She always grumbled about Cassie but now she wished she was in. She needed someone to share this unexpected jubilance. Where had it come from? She paced the little flat, drifting restlessly into each room bar Cassie's, which she had recently started locking when she went out. She did this circuit several times before stopping abruptly in front of the mirror in her own room. She tucked a few straggles of mousy hair behind her ear. What would she look like blonde? She had never dyed her hair. Her mother had said that nice girls, her sort, did not do that sort of thing. Nor did they paint their nails. Or pierce their ears. Flora held out her stubby fingers. She was not a beauty but she wasn't unattractive. She liked her nose. It was delicate and straight with the slightest flare to the nostrils. What would it look like with the tiny twinkle of a stud? She was only plain in that she lacked colour. She blended in with the beige of the walls. Even her eyes were nondescript. Her mother had insisted they were hazel and "interesting" but to her they had always been dun. She ran a brush through her hair, laughing at the static to reveal two large front teeth which even braces hadn't managed to rein in. She reached for her spectacles, small and neat like her room, and pulled on her boots. It was decided. It was time to live. She deliberately left her bed unmade, disregarded the fact that her pyjama bottoms were flung over her chair instead of folded tidily under the pillow. She positively bounced out of the room. Positively positive. Then she ran back in, ran over to the little shelf by the window. She picked up the little figure. Felt its familiar coolness in her hands. She kissed it gently before replacing it on the velvet cloth.

"Gratias tibi ago" she enunciated, suddenly serious. "Intellego" she murmured before dashing off again. I understand. I understand. I know now.

*

"I'll pray for you. Again."
"Huh?"
"You really should try it. Prayer. It helps."
"Helps?"
"Yeah. You're not alone, Flo. A lot of people care about you."
Cassie looked serious. The sunshine had left her face. Her big blue eyes bored into Flora, her eyebrows knitted together. Flora felt restless. Flustered. On edge. Something was happening.
"God loves you. I love…"
"Which one?"
"What?"
"Which god?"
Cassie patted the bed next to her.
"Flora, stop. Sit down."
Flora reshuffled her pile of papers, closed her laptop and did as she was bid.
"Flo, I'm worried about you."
"I'm fine"
Cassie's eyebrows rose.
"Honestly. In fact I'm more than fine. I'm good. Really good."
Cassie looked awkward.
"There's only one God. Why do you ask which?"
"How do you know, Cassie?"
"The Bible."
Flora shook her head. She saw that answer coming.
"There were other religions before Christianity. What about the Romans? They really believed in their gods, just as you are convinced about yours. What has happened to their gods now? Why did people stop worshipping them? Maybe in two thousand years people will have forgotten about Jesus."
Cassie stood up.
"Those gods were false idols. Why don't you actually read the Bible? It's all in there. I have to go. I'm sorry, Flo. I can't do this."

*

Beepbeepbeepbeepbeepbeepbeep! Blackness billowed, gobbling up the living room. Flora's eyes stung and her throat tickled. Never mind. Keep going. She prodded the fire with a metal skewer. The chicken offering she had made had already been consumed but the flames were still famished. She threw on the remains of the newspaper. Whoosh! They snatched it, growing tall. Flora looked about the room. There was a book on the table. The Book. That would do it. But could she? Vesta demanded that the fire be eternal. She tore off her shirt and offered up that instead. She started to cough. Why was there so much smoke? Never mind. Keep going. She fought through the clouds of soot to the kitchen. She grabbed two frying pans and started clanging them together. This flat needed to be cleansed of its lemures for there were many she was sure. Ghosts. Too much sadness. This was the answer. She would get this flat in order and then bring Amy here. Now that she understood, they would get along. They could start afresh. She hadn't felt this good in ages. Her life was really coming together. How long had the alarm been shrieking? Never mind. Keep going. She hurriedly moved about the place, banging. The flat was only small and the blackness was creeping into every room. Back in the hall. Cassie. Open mouthed.

www.ingramcontent.com/pod-product-compliance
Lightning Source LLC
Chambersburg PA
CBHW020134180726
47992CB00022B/2981